UGLY FISH

Kara LaReau Scott Magoon

Harcourt, Inc.
Orlando Austin New York San Diego Toronto London

Requests for permission to make copies of any part of the work should be
mailed to the following address: Permissions Department, Harcourt, Inc.,
6277 Sea Harbor Drive, Orlando, Florida 32887-6777.

www.HarcourtBooks.com

Library of Congress Cataloging-in-Publication Data
LaReau, Kara.
Ugly Fish/Kara LaReau; illustrated by Scott Magoon.
p. cm.
Summary: At first, Ugly Fish likes being alone in his tank so much that he eats
any fish that tries to share it, but when he becomes lonely, he devises a better plan.
[1. Fishes—Fiction. 2. Sharing—Fiction. 3. Loneliness—Fiction.]
I. Magoon, Scott, ill. II. Title.
PZ7.L32078Ug 2006
[E]—dc22   2004024315
ISBN-13: 978-0152-05082-5 ISBN-10: 0-15-205082-5

C E G H F D B

Manufactured in China

The illustrations in this book were done in pen and ink and then digitally colored.
The display type was set in Bokka and digitally altered by Scott Magoon.
The text type was set in Potato Cut and Bokka.
Color Separations by Colourscan Co. Pte. Ltd., Singapore
Manufactured by South China Printing Company, Ltd., China
This book was printed on 120gsm Woodfree Offset Text.
Production Supervision by Ginger Boyer
Designed by Lauren Rille

For all the ugly fish
swimming around out there—
you know who you are
—K.L.

For Owen
—S.M.

Ugly Fish was ugly.
And **BIG**.
And mean.

He liked swimming around
in his fish tank.

He liked gliding in . . .

and out . . .

of his driftwood tunnel.

He liked eating
his special briny flakes.

One day, a new fish appeared in the tank.

"I am Teensy Fish," the new fish said,
flicking his tail fin. "What's your name?"

"I am **UGLY FISH**," said Ugly Fish.
"And there's only room for one fish in *this* tank—**ME!**"

Ugly Fish chased Teensy Fish
around the tank.

And then he ate him.

Another day, another fish appeared in the tank.
"Hello there!" the new fish said, blowing bubbles.
"I am Kissy Fish. What's your name?"

"I am **UGLY FISH**," said Ugly Fish.
"And there's only room for one fish in *this* tank—**ME!**"

Ugly Fish

chased   Kissy Fish

around

the tank.

And then he ate her.

Two days later, two other fish appeared in the tank.
"We are Stripy Fish and Spotty Fish,"
the new fish said. "What's your name?"

"I am **UGLY FISH**," said Ugly Fish.
"And there's only room for one fish in *this* tank—**ME!**"

Ugly Fish chased Stripy Fish and Spotty Fish around the tank.

And then he ate them.

Ugly Fish was very satisfied with himself.
He swam around in his tank, blowing bubbles.

He glided in and out...

in and out...

in and out...of his driftwood tunnel.

He gulped down
his special briny flakes.

But after a while,
the tunnel didn't seem so fun anymore.
The special briny flakes
no longer tasted very special.

Ugly Fish was glum.

I wish I had someone to play with, he thought.

Chasing those fish was fun.

If only I hadn't eaten them.

At last, a new fish appeared in the tank.

Ugly Fish blew bubbles.

His fins perked up.

"Hello there!" he said.
"I am **UGLY FISH**. What's your name?"

"I am Shiny Fish," said the fish.

"Welcome to my tank!" said Ugly Fish,
flicking his tail fin.
"This is my driftwood tunnel."

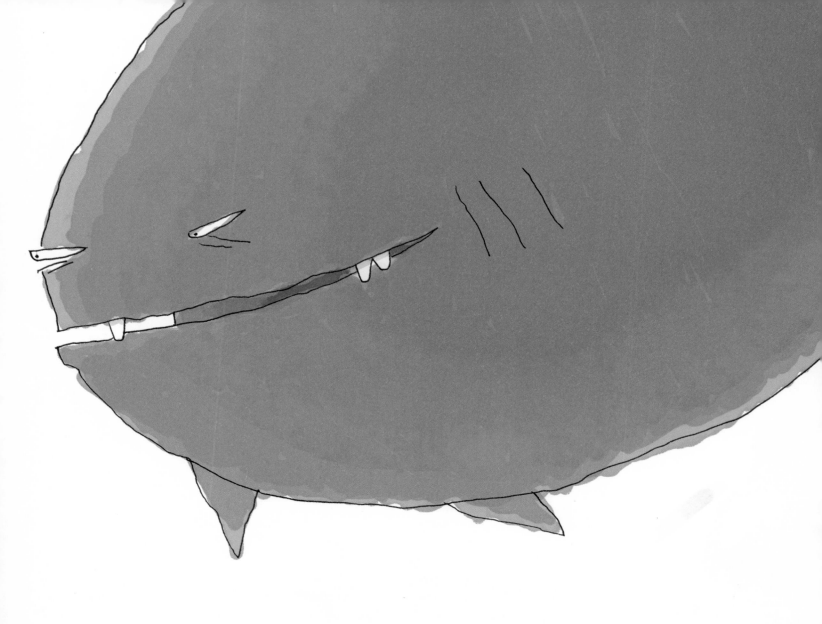

"Nice," said Shiny Fish.

"And these are my special briny flakes,"
said Ugly Fish.

"There's plenty of room for both of us," said Ugly Fish. "Do you like to play?"

"Oh, I like to play," said Shiny Fish. "And then, I like to *eat*."

"That makes two of us!" said Ugly Fish.

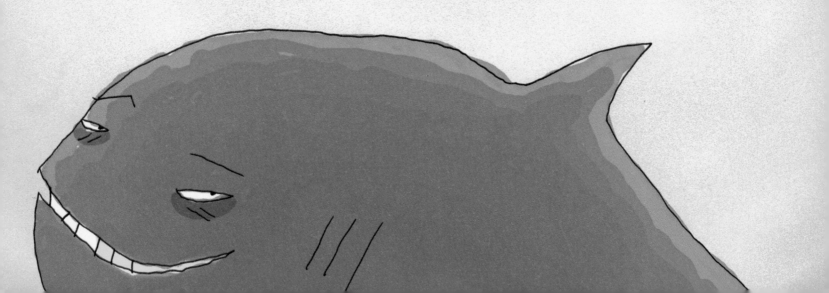

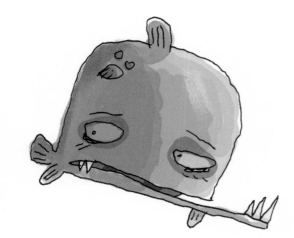

"Guess again," said Shiny Fish.

So Ugly Fish got his wish—

a new friend to play with.

And Shiny Fish got his wish, too—

a nice new home...